Two Naughty Angels

The Ghoul at School

Two Naughty Angels
The Ghoul at School

Mary Hooper

Illustrated by Lesley Harker

BLOOMSBURY

First published in Great Britain in 1995 by Bloomsbury Publishing Plc
36 Soho Square, London, W1D 3QY

This edition first published in 2008

Text copyright © Mary Hooper 1995
Illustrations copyright © Lesley Harker 1995

A CIP catalogue record of this book is available from the
British Library

ISBN 978 0 7475 9060 6

All papers used by Bloomsbury Publishing are natural, recyclable products made
from wood grown in well-managed forests. The manufacturing processes conform
to the environmental regulations of the country of origin.

Typeset by Dorchester Typesetting Group Ltd
Printed in Great Britain by Clays Ltd, St Ives Plc

1 3 5 7 9 10 8 6 4 2

www.bloomsbury.com
www.maryhooper.co.uk

Prologue

In heaven there's a viewing mirror where, every fifty years, angels are allowed to have a glimpse of earth. Angels can't remember anything of their earthly lives – their mums, dads, homes or pets – and so looking through the viewing mirror is always exciting and fascinating.

Heaven may be very beautiful, but all it contains is lots and lots of clouds, and if you're a small and lively angel, it can get a little bit boring. This is why, when the mirror cracked, Gabrielle and Angela jumped through and landed on earth.

They've made a friend, Julia, who knows that they're angels, but no one else at St Winifred's Convent School does.

The angels are having a lot of fun living like ordinary schoolgirls and want to stay. But the Archangel wants them back in heaven . . .

1

One of Your Wings Is Showing . . .

It was evening and Gabrielle and Angela were in the small bathroom next to their dormitory in St Winifred's. The bell for bedtime had already rung and Angie (who always kept to the Heavenly Angels' Code of Conduct) had cleaned her teeth until they shone like pearls. She was about to go into the dorm and get into bed when Gaby stopped her.

'Hang on,' she said. 'One of your wings is showing. Here!' She tucked a few stray feathers under Angie's nightie and inside her vest. 'That's better.

We wouldn't want Marcy to see anything suspicious, would we?'

'No, we wouldn't,' Angie said, doing up the top button on her nightie. 'She's already watching us like a hook.'

'Not a hook – a *hawk*,' Gaby corrected. 'It's a bird.'

'Is that like a budgie?'

'Sort of,' Gaby said. She took a nervous look at the mirror. 'Don't let's hang around in here – the Archangel may be looking out for us.'✯

Angie and Gaby shared their dorm with five other First Year girls: Julia (their special friend), Sarah, Susie, Nicola and, unfortunately, Marcy.

When they were all in bed and the bell for Lights Out had sounded, Miss Bunce, their form mistress, put her head around the door. Miss Bunce was old, thin as a stick and usually draped in coloured scarves and shawls.

✯ When the angels are alone, the Archangel sometimes appears in a mirror to urge them to return to heaven.

'Now, girls,' she said, peering at them over her little round glasses and adjusting three scarves, 'I want you to go straight to sleep. We don't want any silliness tonight.'

Angie put her head out from under her duvet. 'Yes, we do!' she said. 'I like silliness! That's when we bounce about on the beds and have pillow fights and make a noise, isn't it?'

Gaby, in the next bed, stretched out her arm and poked at Angie to get her to shut up. 'Do be quiet!' she angel-whispered. 'You don't say things like that to a teacher!'※

'I'm just telling the truth,' Angie angel-whispered back, 'like I always do.'

'Well, I wish you wouldn't!'

'If you'd been to Halo Awareness Classes then *you'd* always want to tell the truth, too!' Angie said.

'You're not going on about those again!' said Gaby.

Fortunately, because Miss Bunce was slightly deaf, she hadn't heard what Angie had said about bed-bouncing. She went on: 'We don't want any silliness, girls, because tomorrow morning our dear Mother Superior arrives back in the convent and we must all be up early, bright-eyed and eager, to meet her. She's rather strict so it'll be excellent behaviour and best foot forward!'

※ Angels can speak to each other in very low voices so that no one else can hear.

'Which is my best foot?' Angie asked. 'Mine both look the same.' She pulled up her duvet and stared down at her toes. 'Most bits of you are the same,  aren't they? Eyes and legs and hands and wi—'

'Where has Mother Superior been?' Gaby quickly interrupted. Since the beginning of term, Mother Superior, the head teacher of the school, had been away. The new First Years had never seen her; all they'd seen was her grim, unsmiling portrait hanging in the school hall.

'On an educational course,' Miss Bunce said. 'A special course concerning religion and how one can promote heavenly feelings.'

Both angels looked at each other.

'What are heavenly feelings exactly?' Gaby asked innocently.

'Oh – just to do with being nice to each other, I expect,' Miss Bunce said vaguely. 'No doubt we'll be hearing all about it. Now, straight to sleep!' she warned as she went out.

The minute she closed the door, Sarah sat up.

'Don't go to sleep, anyone,' she said importantly. 'My sister Hannah is coming along in a minute and she's got something exciting to tell us.'

The girls talked among themselves for a while but Hannah – a Fourth Year – was such a long time coming that Susie had fallen asleep by the time she arrived and had to be woken up.

'I couldn't get out before!' Hannah puffed, out of breath from having run up the eighty steps to the top of the tower where the First Years' dorm was. She plonked herself down on Sarah's bed. 'Sister Gerty has got wind that something's up. She was hanging around outside our dorm for ages, then luckily someone called her away and I just got out and flew straight up here.'

The younger girls looked at her with interest, wondering what it was she'd come to tell them. Only Angie was frowning.

'You didn't really fly,' she said, 'because you

can't. Only *angels* can fly.'

'That's just an expression,' Gaby said quickly, before Angie could drop them right in it. 'Anyway, lots of things can fly: birds and butterflies and moths and –'

'*Us!*' said Angie in an angel-whisper.

'Oh, do go on, Hannah!' Julia said. 'What's the big secret?'

Hannah looked round, enjoying the drama. She lowered her voice to a hoarse whisper. 'I came to warn you that . . . the ghost has been seen again!' she said, and all the girls – except the angels – gave little screams of fright.

'I d-didn't know there was a ghost here!' Susie stuttered. 'I wouldn't have come to this school if I'd known there was a ghost.'

'Is it a real ghost?' Julia asked nervously. 'Is it all dressed in white?'

'Does it walk through walls?' Sarah asked.

'Does it rattle ghostly chains?' Nicola wanted to know.

'It's a ghost called the Blue Nun,' Hannah said in a spooky voice. 'She haunts the main hallways, drifting up and down the stairs scaring people.' She rolled her eyes as if she was terrified. 'They say she appears whenever there's going to be trouble at school!'

Most of the girls had disappeared beneath their duvets by this time, but Angie and Gaby sat up and looked at Hannah with interest.

9

'I wouldn't be scared of a ghost,' Angie said carelessly. 'Ghosts are just like angels.'

'They're only a *bit* like angels,' Gaby said, and added to Angie in a rather superior angel-whisper, 'they're on a lower level of heaven to us.'

'I know! They're from Level Two,' Angie whispered back.

'I don't believe in them!' said Marcy, who'd been listening carefully up till then. 'And even if there are such things, they wouldn't frighten *me*!'

'Well, I think they're scary!' Julia said, from under her duvet.

'So do I,' Nicola said. 'I don't want to meet one!'

'That's why I thought I'd warn you,' Hannah said. 'You should keep to your dorms after Lights Out and if you have to go anywhere, go in pairs.'

She jumped off Sarah's bed. 'I'd better go. I want to frighten . . . er . . . tell the other First Years about the ghost before Sister Gerty gets back.'

When she'd gone to the other dorm, the girls talked amongst themselves in nervous whispers until, one by one, they fell asleep.

'That's an Archangel, a Mother Superior and a ghost to watch out for,' Gaby said to Angie just before she snuggled down. 'We're going to be busy.'

2

The Angels Sigh Up a Storm

'What do you think she'll be like?' Angie asked Gaby the following morning as they filed into the hall.

'The ghost?'

'No, that other person. The other superior.'

'*Mother* Superior,' said Gaby. She nodded towards the black-habited nuns sitting each side of the hall. 'I expect she'll just be like all the other nuns. Perhaps a bit older.'

Angie stared at the large and forbidding portrait of Mother Superior hanging over the stage at the

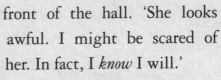

front of the hall. 'She looks awful. I might be scared of her. In fact, I *know* I will.'

'She'll probably be strict — like Sister Gertrude.'

'Sarah said that she's a nogar!' Angie said.

'What's a nogar?' Gaby asked.

Julia, beside them, giggled. 'An *ogre*. That just means she's very fierce.'

Miss Bunce, wrapped in purple and red scarves, waved at them from her chair. '*Do* be quiet, First Years!' she hissed. 'Our Mother Superior will be here directly and she'll want absolute silence.'

Suddenly, there was a jingling and a strumming and a tinkling noise offstage, then a small fat figure appeared. The small fat figure was dressed in a nun's habit which had been cut short to reveal pink-striped socks and ankle boots. Mother

Superior had been on a course with a difference.

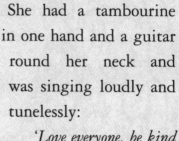 She had a tambourine
in one hand and a guitar
round her neck and
was singing loudly and
tunelessly:

'*Love everyone, be kind
and true,*
*That's what we
should try to do!*'

As she barked out the
words she jumped from one foot to the other,
shaking the tambourine with her right hand and
strumming the guitar with her left.

'That doesn't look very fierce,' Angie remarked.
'Not like a nogar.'

'Sssshh!' said Gaby. 'Look at all the other nuns!'

The nuns – and everyone else in the hall who'd
known Mother Superior before she'd been on the
course – were staring open-mouthed at the figure
on the stage.

Mother Superior paused, panting heavily. 'Ah!'

she said, 'I thought that might surprise you! Let me tell you, girls, that I have seen the light!' She cleared her throat and crashed the tambourine on to her knee:

'No more hard words, no more stress,
Mother Superior brings happiness!'

Gaby and Angie, used to pure and beautiful angel voices, shrank down and put their hands over their ears.

Mother Superior went on to explain in awful sing-song verse that she wasn't going to be strict ever again. She was going to love everyone and be wonderful to everyone all the time. And while she was being wonderful, she was going to sing about it.

'I've composed a new St Winifred's school song and I want you all to learn the chorus and clap along with me!' she brayed, while the whole school stared at her, dumbfounded. She shook the tambourine again and clanged a bell hanging by her side:

'*So ring, ring, ring that bell,*

Let's banish every thought of hell!'

'Bless you!' the angels chorused.✭

Julia turned to Gaby and Angie. 'Oh, no,' she muttered.

'Once more. All together now!' Mother Superior shrieked. 'Clap along in time!'

The bewildered school sang it again, and the angels again cried, '*Bless you!'*

Marcy turned to stare. 'You two – why on earth do you keep saying that?'

'Because I keep sneezing,' Julia said quickly.

'I haven't heard you.'

'That's because I always do very quiet sneezes. Like this: *Atishoo! Atishoo!'* she sneezed softly. 'Oops, there I go again!'

After several more choruses (and lots more *bless*

✭ Whenever the word 'hell' is mentioned, angels are programmed to say 'bless you'.

*you*s from the angels followed by quiet sneezes from Julia), Mother Superior danced herself offstage, exhausted. While the school sat, stunned, Sister Bertha, one of the older nuns, went to the piano and started playing a normal hymn.

It was one that the angels knew and they sang along, their voices rising clear and pure and distinct from everyone else's — not surprising considering that they'd been practising in a heavenly choir for two hundred and forty-seven years. They sounded *so* beautiful that several girls around them stopped singing and listened entranced.

'Your singing of our last hymn today, girls, was most melodic,' Miss Bunce said when they were all back in class. 'It was quite delightful. You sang like nightingales or . . .'

'Or like angels?' Gaby asked.

'No one can sing quite that well,' Miss Bunce said gently. She got out her needlework. 'Now, as our . . . er . . . dear Mother Superior has kept us in assembly longer than usual, there won't be time for your English Grammar lesson.' She glanced out of the window. 'You might go outside for a game of netball, perhaps . . .'

Gaby and Angie looked at each other and pulled faces.

'Or does it look like rain?' Miss Bunce went on, peering up at the sky.

Gaby poked Angie, and they nodded at each other.✱

'Oh, dear Miss Bunce,' Angie sighed, '*please* don't make us go out and do games.'

Now Gaby moaned low and long. 'Games are *awful*.'

'Horrible . . .'

✱ When an angel sighs, storm clouds gather in the sky. Two or more angels can create quite a rain storm.

'Awfully horrible . . .' said Gaby, heaving another huge sigh.

'Dear me!' said Miss Bunce, looking outside again. 'It's suddenly got much darker. It's actually started raining now.'

'May we go to the common room instead?' Julia asked.

'We'll be very quiet. And then you could get on with your lovely needlework,' Gaby added persuasively.

In a trice, Miss Bunce had pulled out her beaded lace milk-jug covers and was bent over them. 'Off you go, then!' she said.

Julia and Angie were first into the common room.

'You won't be able to do that sighing business too often, you know,' Julia said, 'or you'll send the rainwater level up for this area.'

'What does that mean?'

'Well, say it usually rains an average of three centimetres for September and you –'

Angie gave a sudden scream and clutched at

Julia's arm, pointing at the object on the corner table.

'Ooh! You've got a viewing mirror in here!' she shrieked. 'The Archangel must have sent it! He's come to get us back!'

And she turned and ran as fast as she could back down the corridor to tell Gaby.

3

Another Viewing Mirror?

'There's a viewing mirror . . . the Archangel . . . he's come to get us back!' Angie cried, jumping up and down in front of Gaby. 'Oh, what shall we do?'

'What do you mean?' Gaby asked. 'What are you talking about?'

'In the common room! A viewing mirror!' Angie wailed. 'Oh, he must be awfully cross with us!' Tears welled up in her eyes. 'He'll make us go back through it and then we'll be sent to a lower level of heaven and –'

'Ssshh!' said Gaby. 'Calm down. Don't let anyone –'

But Marcy had already heard some of the commotion. 'There's always something odd going on when you two are around,' she said. 'What's the fuss about now?'

Julia ran up behind Angie, panting. 'It's all right,' she said. 'Angie was . . . er . . . just a bit frightened about something.'

'What?' demanded Marcy.

Julia bit her lip. 'Well the . . . er . . . television, actually.'

'The television!' Marcy said scornfully. 'How can anyone be frightened of a television?'

'She hasn't seen one before,' Julia said. 'They don't have them where she comes from.'

'Don't *have* them?!' Marcy exclaimed.

Angie was still uttering little squeals of panic. 'Whatever Julia calls it, it's still a viewing mirror,' she angel-whispered to Gaby. 'It's got moving pictures on it!'

'It's all right,' Julia said. 'It can't hurt you,

22

honestly it can't. Come and see.'

'We'll go and have a look,' Gaby said, and added in an angel-whisper to Angie, 'If we see the Archangel in it, we'll run away.'

They walked back down the corridor towards the common room, Julia leading the way and Marcy, a spiteful, scornful look on her face, bringing up the rear.

Julia pushed open the door. 'There it is,' she said. 'It's called a television. It's been away for repair and they've only just brought it back.'

The two angels peered cautiously round the door, ready to take flight at a second's notice.

'Wh-what's that in it?' Gaby asked.

'Who's that funny little person?'

Angie asked tremulously.

'Peter Rabbit,' Julia said. 'It's a story about a . . . er . . . little furry thing a bit like a cat.'

'Don't tell me they don't know what rabbits are!' Marcy said.

Gaby and Angie had taken small steps into the common room and were staring, entranced, at the television.

'What's *that*?' Angie asked.

'That's the weather man,' Julia said.

'And now . . . ?' Gaby and Angie were sitting inches from the set by then, watching every flicker and movement.

'And that . . . and that . . . ?'

'That's an advertisement for toothpaste, and *that's* one for a car, and *that's* a cowboy and . . . oh,' Julia said, 'I think I'm going to be here all day.'

'And I think you're seriously weird,' Marcy said to the angels.

'Do you two weirdos ever have a shower?' Marcy asked the angels that evening. The two of them were last up to the dorm – Julia had only just managed to prise them away from the TV.

'That's nothing to do with you,' Gaby said.

'Only dirty people shower,' said Angie.

'I don't think you've got undressed since you've been here,' Marcy went on. 'Either that or you shower with your vests on.'

Gaby and Angie didn't say anything, just smiled and tossed their ringlets. Marcy had actually hit the nail on the head: to make sure the feathers on

25

their wings didn't get too wet, the angels always whizzed under the shower wearing their vests, then changed into dry ones.

'Do stop going on, Marcy,' Julia said. 'They're just different from us, that's all. They have different customs. Maybe they're too shy to take their vests off in front of anyone else.'

'Hmm,' said Marcy suspiciously.

A while later, Angie was scrubbing her nails at the sink, and Gaby was in one of the shower cubicles having a quick splash – with her vest on, of course. Suddenly Marcy ran in past Angie and crashed against the shower cubicle door.

'I've got you trapped!' Marcy shouted over the partition. 'I'm sitting here and blocking the door until you come out. *And* I've got your clean vest and nightie!'

Gaby carried on showering, smiling an angelic smile to herself.

'You can't get out of there unless you go past me!' Marcy called.

'If I can't go past you, I'll have to go *over* you,' Gaby said.

'What's that supposed to mean?'

'Oh, nothing!' said Gaby, and she angel-whispered to Angie, 'Have you got a good pinch of angel dust handy?' ✱

'I'll look in a minute,' Angie angel-whispered back. She inspected her nails carefully. '*Nails well scrubbed, hands all clean, Show an angel's bright and keen* – I learnt that in my last Halo Awareness Class.'

'Never mind that! Hurry up!'

'OK! Cavalry to the rescue!' called Angie, who'd just been watching a cowboy film on TV.

She peered round the corner and, taking a good pinch of angel dust, blew it into Marcy's eyes.

Marcy yawned twice and then closed her eyes and gently slid right down on to the floor.

✱ In heaven, angel dust is used to send crying cherubs off to sleep. Angels always keep some in their pockets, just in case.

'She's sleeping like a cherub,'
Angie called to Gaby. 'But
she's still blocking the door.'

'It's just as well I can fly
then, isn't it?' Gaby said,
and she flapped her wings
once, twice, and was over
the door of the shower
cubicle in an instant. 'Is it a bird, is
it a plane — no, it's an angel!' she cried (she'd been
watching *Superman*).

'Thank you so much for keeping my vest and
nightie for me,' she said, taking them from the
sleeping Marcy.

'And we wish you a very good night,' added
Angie as they both went out.

Two hours later, Marcy awoke stiff and cold on the
bathroom floor and blundered into the dorm,
waking everyone up.

'What happened? What was I doing on the
floor?' she asked crossly, rubbing her eyes.

'What is it?' Sarah called. 'Who's that? Is it the ghost?'

'No, it's Marcy,' said Angie. 'She's been having a nice sleep on the bathroom floor.'

'Something funny's going on,' Marcy said, standing over Gaby's bed and glowering at her. 'How did you get out of that cubicle?'

'I just opened the door and out I came!' said Gaby.

Marcy narrowed her eyes. 'So why is the door still locked?'

'Ah,' said Gaby, looking thoughtful.

'Maybe the ghost of the Blue Nun has been walking,' said Julia. 'Maybe she locked it.'

'Maybe she has,' Gaby said.

'Night, everyone!' both angels called into the darkness.

4

The Peter Rabbit Stew

'There you are at last!' said the Archangel rather crossly. 'I've been looking out of mirrors for an age without finding you.'

As the Archangel, clothed all in white, appeared in a blaze of light in the bathroom mirror, both angels jumped back.

'Just when we thought it was safe to go back in front of a mirror,' muttered Gaby.

'We haven't been around much because we've been watching a lot of television,' Angie said. 'Do you know what that is? It's really exciting – you

30

get to see squillions of things.'

'It might be an idea to get one for heaven,' Gaby said. 'Stop it getting quite so boring,' she added in an angel-whisper to Angie, quite forgetting that the Archangel could hear her.

But he had other things on his mind. 'I really haven't the time to fly around after you at the moment,' he said sternly. 'I'm far too busy. They've put Yours Gloriously in complete charge of a whole new faction of saints and seraphs.'

Angie, who was trying to hide behind Gaby, nudged her in the back to speak.

'Oh, *do* let us stay just a little longer,' Gaby said.

'You are not supposed to be here at all,' the Archangel insisted. 'How are you ever to learn to be exalted and wondrous and proceed up the celestial ladder to higher levels if you remaineth on earth?'

'Oh, just a bit longer,' Angie

piped up, 'because in this TV series we're watching there's a boy in hospital and we don't know whether he'll live or die and if he does die I want to see if he turns into an angel and –'

'No, I must insist that –' the Archangel began, and then suddenly Julia crashed through the bathroom door and instantly he disappeared.

'Phew!' Gaby said.

'Saved by the Julia,' said Angie.

'There you are! Come on!' Julia said. 'I've been waiting for you so we can go into lunch. I thought you'd be in the common room – this is the first time I've seen you away from the TV since it arrived!'

'You just missed the Archangel,' Gaby said. 'We've been having a lecture from him.'

'Oh, wow!' Julia said. 'I would've liked to have seen an Archangel.'

'Never mind,' Angie said comfortingly. 'You can see him when you're dead.'

'*You've* just missed Mother Superior,' said Julia. 'She's been jigging around in the dining hall, singing lots of choruses of the new school song with plenty of mentions of . . . er . . . you know where.'

Angie shuddered. 'I hate her voice. I have to put my hands over my ears when I hear her.'

'Well, it's all right – she's gone for her own lunch now,' said Julia. 'And I'm starving. Are you coming?'

'Affirmative!' said Angie.

'Bet your bottom dollar!' said Gaby.

Julia groaned. 'You two! Talk about TV addicts.'

In the dining hall, the three friends queued for food with the other girls. The angels looked expectantly towards a big, steaming casserole of something being dished out by Mrs Smithers, the chief dinner-lady.✷

'I hope there's a lot,' Angie said as they lined up. 'What is it?' she asked when they reached Mrs Smithers, who was standing with her ladle.

'Stew,' Mrs Smithers said. 'Rabbit stew.'

✷ The angels love food. In heaven all they had was a small goblet of milk and honey each day.

'*Rabbit* stew?' Angie said in horror. 'One of those darling little Peter Rabbits in a stew?'

'Well, er . . .'

'Still with all his fur and whiskers?' Gaby asked.

'Not exactly . . .'

'And his braces and little blue trousers?' Angie anguished. 'Oh, no! I could never eat a Peter Rabbit in a stew.'

'Sshh!' said Mrs Smithers.

'Nor me! And I couldn't eat a boiled Benjamin Bunny either – I'd rather die,' said Gaby, temporarily forgetting that she was already dead.

'Do please keep your opinions to yourself,' whispered Mrs Smithers. It was too late, though – Julia and the two girls behind her had already turned down the stew and picked up a cheese salad.

The words 'Peter Rabbit stew' and 'boiled Benjamin Bunny' spread down the line and suddenly no one in the queue wanted anything hot. Girls who already had the stew on their plate pushed it to one side, others were asked by Angie if they would please join her campaign to 'Ban Eating Bunnies.' Mrs  Smithers was left with a very large portion of rabbit stew to take home, and decided there and then to put a vegetarian dish on the menu every day.

'What a lot of fuss you two made at lunchtime,' Marcy said when the girls were getting ready for bed that evening. 'I can't see what's wrong with eating rabbit or pig or lamb or anything else.'

'You wouldn't,' Gaby said in an angel-whisper. 'I expect you'd eat one of those cats given half a chance.'

Nicola, who was standing near her locker, gave a sudden gasp. 'Hey! My chocolates have gone!'

'What chocolates?' Sarah asked.

'The special box of mint creams I was keeping. I was just letting myself have one chocolate a night.'

Marcy pointed at the angels. 'They like chocolates.'

'That's not fair,' Julia said immediately. 'We *all* like chocolates.'

Marcy walked round Gaby's bed and opened her locker. 'Where did you get all this stuff?' she asked, looking at the hairbrush and various sprays and lotions that were inside. She pointed at Angie. 'And what about all the stuff *you've* got? I thought your suitcases got lost on their way here.'

'I've been giving them some things of mine,' Julia said quickly. 'And Matron has, too.'

'Matron told us we could take some things from Lost Properly,' Angie said.

Julia giggled. 'Lost *Property*,' she corrected.

'Aren't they lost properly, then?' Angie asked innocently.

Everyone laughed – except Marcy. 'So who's taken the chocolates?'

'Oh, they're not important,' said Nicola. 'Let's forget about them.'

'My sister told me the ghost of the Blue Nun has been seen again,' Sarah said. 'Perhaps *she's* moved them.'

'Hmm,' said Marcy. 'I don't think ghosts eat chocolates. I think it was someone a *lot closer*. And I'm going to be watching both of those someones very carefully indeed from now on . . .'

5

Angie Tells Mother Superior the Truth

'Look! The Archangel!' Gaby said to Angie the following morning in the school chapel.

'He's not here *again*?!' Angie said in a panic. '*Where?*'

Gaby pointed. 'Over there.'

'I can't see him. Is there a viewing mirror in here, then?'

'Of course not,' Gaby laughed. 'It's a joke. There's a picture of an archangel in stained glass – on that window there next to some saints and a pair of golden gates.'

'Oh, honestly!' Angie said. She looked at the chapel window and screwed up her nose. 'It doesn't look a bit like our Archangel. He's not old enough and anyway, he wouldn't be seen dead – oops!' She giggled. 'I mean, he wouldn't be seen *alive* in a blue cloak. And his wings are all wrong.'

'I suppose that was the best they could do,' Gaby said. 'Considering they can't have seen one.'

'Our next hymn,' Sister Bertha announced from the front steps, 'is number four hundred and five. And I'd like to hear some lovely singing from the First Year girls, please.'

The organ played the first few chords and the girls started singing. Gaby and Angie joined in and their angel voices soared effortlessly above those of the others.

Sister Bertha listened for a moment, head on one side, looking startled, then came down towards the First Years and began to walk between the lines, listening intently.

As she neared where they were standing, Julia nudged Gaby. 'Be quiet – stop singing or alter your voices or something!' she whispered. 'Sister Bertha is on to you!'

The angels, whose voices had been finely tuned, were able to drop suddenly to the bottom of the scale and sing very low, almost gruffly. They did this as Sister Bertha approached and she reached the end of their line looking puzzled.

'This is most peculiar,' she mused when the hymn had finished. 'Perhaps it was just the wind blowing through the trees outside . . .'

'What was, Sister Bertha?' Julia asked.

'Well, as you were all singing that hymn, I heard . . . well, you may laugh, children, but I thought I heard some beautiful voices – like a heavenly choir!'

The girls *did* laugh. Especially three of them.

'But when I walked along the lines, I couldn't hear anything unusual at all.' She smiled gently. 'I think I must have heard something other-worldly . . .'

There was a jingling and a strumming from outside and the girls shifted uneasily.

'Ah, our dear Mother Superior is joining us for a song,' said Sister Bertha, trying to sound pleased as the small, squat figure in white furry bootees bounced in.

'Children!' Mother Superior beamed, shaking her tambourine enthusiastically. 'I've come along to sing you one or two of my latest numbers, and then we're all going to sing the school song!'

Most of the girls groaned quietly to themselves

and Julia's heart sank, knowing she'd have to do a lot of pretend-sneezing. Looking anguished, Angie put her hands tightly over her ears.

Mother Superior noticed. 'The little girl in the front row — what is it? Have you got earache?'

Angie shook her head. 'Oh, no, it's not that.'

'Why are you covering your ears then, my child?'

'Because your voice is so awful,' Angie replied politely. 'I would have earache if I had to listen to it for long. And a headache too, I should think.'

Mother Superior gasped and dropped her tambourine. There was a shocked silence from the others. Even Gaby, used to Angie telling the truth at all times, was stunned.

'Perhaps you could have singing lessons,' Angie suggested politely. 'Then we wouldn't all shudder when you come in.'

'You've done it now,' Gaby said in an angel-whisper.

Mother Superior slowly picked up her tambourine from the floor.

'I think the child must be delirious!' Sister Bertha said quickly. 'She doesn't know what she's saying.'

'Oh, I think she does,' Mother Superior said, and everyone held their breath. She went on: 'And it is quite wonderful that she felt she was able to say it.' She clasped her hands together. 'From this dear child has come the genuine, unvarnished truth. This child has the honesty and purity of an angel!'

Everyone in the chapel turned to stare at Angie.

'Well, now you've said that, Mother Superior, I can see that she even looks a bit like an angel!' Sister Bertha cooed. 'Those golden ringlets . . . that sweet smile . . .'

'Now, see what you've done!' Gaby angel-whispered to Angie. 'They're going to find out about us and then we'll be investigated.' She glanced upwards. 'And I can see a little bit of glitter above

43

your head — your halo is coming back!'✻

Angie thought quickly. It went against all she'd learnt in heaven, but she took a deep breath, screwed up her face and poked her tongue out at Mother Superior, then turned and ran from the room. Thinking that that might not be quite  naughty enough, she kicked Marcy's leg as she passed her.

Gaby noticed with satisfaction that by the time Angie reached the door, her halo had quite disappeared.

✻ The angels lost their haloes when they came down to earth. If they ever do anything especially good, though, they begin to reappear.

There was a bit of a fuss, of course, but it was such a very odd school anyway that one pupil's strange behaviour didn't merit a lot of attention. Later that day, however, Mother Superior announced that she was having singing lessons and started composing a new song in honour of the occasion. The first line came to her easily and went: '*Always tell the truth, truth, truth!*' but after that she got a bit stuck. Going past her door that afternoon, the girls heard her strumming her guitar and muttering: '*Truth, truth, truth!* . . . Um . . . booth, forsooth, tooth, uncouth, youth, Ruth . . .'

When the girls went up to their dorm that evening, Sarah's sister Hannah was waiting for them.

'My class has been out on a trip all day,' she said, 'so I couldn't tell you the news before.'

'Is it about the ghost?' said Angie.

'Has she been haunting again?' Sarah asked eagerly.

Hannah nodded. Her voice sank to a husky,

spooky whisper. 'The Blue Nun was seen on the stairs last night!'

'Oh, what time?' Gaby asked, interested.

'Is it always the same place?' asked Angie.

Hannah, rather miffed because the two girls didn't seem in the least bit frightened, replied, 'On the witching hour of midnight! That's when all ghosts walk.'

'Do they?' Gaby asked. 'Well, I think I might go along tonight and have a chat.'

'You wouldn't!' Nicola said.

'Bet I would,' said Gaby.

Susie turned from putting something away in her locker. 'Well, if you do see the ghost, ask her if she's taken the packet of chocolate biscuits I brought from home. They've disappeared!'

'I think I know who is taking things,' Marcy said, 'And it's certainly not a ghost . . .'

6

The Angels and the Ghost

The two angels waited until the rest of the girls in the dorm were asleep, then slid out of bed and made for the door.

'Let's put on our angel nighties and fly down,' Gaby said. 'My wings could do with a bit of exercise. I'm sure it's not doing them any good being squashed under a vest all the time.'

'Groom them, spread them, make them sleek, Take lots of pride in your wings all week!' Angie chanted.

'Don't tell me – Halo Awareness Classes,' Gaby said. 'Come on, let's go!'

Quickly they changed into the nighties they'd been wearing when they arrived from heaven.✻

Slipping out of the dorm door, they floated over the top bannister and played 'It,' darting up and down out of each other's grasp as they soared down the stairs to the bottom of the tower.

Once there, they flew swiftly along the main corridor of the school towards the entrance hall, where Hannah had told them that the ghost of the Blue Nun had been seen.

Angie pointed upwards. 'There she is, hovering over the first landing!'

As quickly as she'd been spotted, the Blue Nun spotted them and raised her arms in the traditional

---

✻ Heavenly nighties always have special wing openings to enable angels to fly more easily.

spooky and ghostly way, uttering little cries of 'Whoo-oo.'

'She's a bit like that ghost in the cartoon!' Angie cried.

'But not nearly so frightening,' said Gaby.

The ghost dropped her arms. 'Who are *you*?' she asked indignantly. 'And if you can see me, why aren't you scared?'

Angie and Gaby zipped upwards at speed and landed on each side of her.

The figure raised her arms for another try. 'Whoo-ooo! I am the ghost of the Blue Nun!' she cried desperately.

'Ghosts aren't as pretty as us!' Angie said, examining the pale figure critically.

'No ringlets!'

'No wings!'

'Different level of heaven, you see,' Gaby finished with a shake of the head.

The ghost sniffed. 'Oh,

you're angels, are you?' she said.

'Gabrielle and Angela,' Gaby said. 'Pleased to meet you.'

'I've never seen angels here before,' said the Blue Nun grumpily. 'I'm sure it's against the rules. How did you arrive?'

'We jumped through the viewing mirror,' Gaby said.

'And the Archangel's trying to get us back,' went on Angie. 'But what are *you* doing here?'

'Just hanging around haunting.'

'What's that like?'

'Bit boring, actually,' the Blue Nun sighed. 'I've been haunting here for nearly a hundred and fifty years but it's only now and again that someone actually sees me. And when they *do* see me they just run away screaming. The cats know I'm here, but they don't like me. I haven't had a decent chat to anyone since 1873.'

'So why do you stay?' Gaby asked. 'Why don't you just go back up to heaven?'

'I can't – I'm stuck,' the Nun said. 'Besides, no

one's even asked for me up there. They haven't got the same tight security on my level of heaven, you see. If we want to drift away, we just do.'

'So now you're here for ever?'

The Nun nodded. 'I suppose I am. Still, it's not too bad,' she rallied. 'Occasionally someone sees me and makes a big fuss, then they sprinkle holy water over me to try to get rid of me – that's fun. It could be worse,' she finished bravely.

'It doesn't *sound* much fun,' said Gaby.

'D'you want us to come and see you again?' Angie asked.

'I wouldn't mind,' said the Blue Nun. 'But if you do, do me a favour – if you've got anyone else with you, try and look a bit frightened. Scaring people is the only fun I get.'

'We will,' promised Angie.

'We'll look *terrified*,' said Gaby as they flew off.

'We saw the ghost,' Angie said to Julia the next morning at breakfast. 'We went and talked to her.'

Julia shuddered. 'Was she awful and scary? Was

she dressed all in white and did she have her head under her arm?'

'I don't *think* so,' Angie said. She turned to Gaby. 'The Blue Nun didn't have her head under her arm, did she?'

''Course she didn't!' Gaby scoffed, munching mushrooms on toast. 'She was quite ordinary. Just a bit thin – you could see the bannisters through her.'

'Well, I don't want to see her. I don't like ghosts and . . .' Julia shuddered again, '. . . dead things.'

'We're dead and you like us,' Gaby pointed out.

'You're different,' said Julia.

'Prettier,' put in Angie.

After breakfast, half of Form 1C went straight to Sister Bridget's class for Home Economics.

Sister Bridget was covered in flour and rather preoccupied with making tasty titbits for a tea party that

Mother Superior was holding that afternoon. She waved the girls in the direction of a pile of cookery books.

'Divide into twos, read up a recipe and make some small cakes of your choice,' she said, wafting more flour around. 'Basic ingredients are in the cupboard. Do your mixing and call me to put the cakes in the oven for you.'

Licking butter from her fingers, she went to the far end of the room and started cutting out cheese pastry into tambourine- and guitar-shaped pieces.

Gaby and Angie pored over cookery books, hesitating over every colourful and chocolatey one they came to. As soon as they saw *angel cakes*, though, they knew what they had to make . . .

Whisking the butter and sugar took only a moment, and the flour and the rest of the ingredients mixed in as easily as anything. 'Just like sifting air,' Angie said.

Gaby dropped spoonfuls of the mixture into twenty little paper cups and they called Sister

Bridget to put the baking tray in the oven. She said they looked extremely light and fluffy, but the first the angels knew that something a bit funny had happened was when Gaby peered in through the door of the oven to see if the cakes were cooked.

She gave a shriek and the other girls looked at her.

'What's up?' Susie asked.

'Nothing!' Gaby said quickly, and she moved in front of the oven so that no one could see through the glass door.

'What is it?' Angie asked in an angel-whisper.

'The cakes!' Gaby whispered back. 'They're so light they've taken off!'

Angie bent to look in. She saw twenty little angel cakes bobbing about two or three centimetres above the baking tray. One or two really light ones had even floated up to the top of the oven. 'They're *flying*!' Angie squeaked.

The angels looked at each other.

'What shall we do?' Gaby asked.

'We could eat them all before anyone sees them,' suggested Angie.

Gaby puffed out her cheeks. 'I don't think even I could eat ten cakes!' She looked along the worktops to where the other girls were putting the finishing touches to their cake mixtures. 'I've got an idea,' she said. 'Can you go and get that big jar of glacé cherries . . .'

They worked swiftly as a team: Angie opened the oven door, Gaby grabbed a cake, stuck five glacé cherries on it to weigh it down, then put it on to a cooling tray.

When Sister Bridget came over a bit later to inspect what the girls had made, she said the angel cakes were the most delicious, fluffy, light-as-a-feather cakes she'd ever tasted. They didn't need glacé cherries on them, she added, they were quite delicious enough without them.

It was only when they were going to their next class that Angie happened to look up at the ceiling, to see that a small, escaped angel cake was bobbing around on the strip-light . . .

7

The Cross-Country Fly

It was Saturday morning, eleven o'clock, and the angels were stretched out on their tummies on the floor of the common room, watching TV and arguing gently about whose turn it was to get up and switch over to the other channel.

Julia, who was on her way to post a letter, popped her head round the door.

'Are you *still* watching that?' she said. 'I've changed my bed, done some prep and written a letter home.'

Angie sat up, dislodging Tiblet the cat who'd

discovered her wings and had taken to sitting on her back snuggled between them.

'We could do that!' she said. 'We could write home to the Archangel.'

'Don't you think delivery might be a bit of a problem?' said Gaby.

Angie frowned. 'I hadn't thought of that.'

'While you're standing there, could you change channels for us?' Gaby asked Julia. 'There's a programme about dinosaurs and –'

The door was suddenly flung open and Sister Teresa, their Sports and PE teacher, stood there jogging up and down on the spot.

'There you are!' she said. 'Fancy watching TV on a lovely morning like this!'

Angie smiled angelically at Sister Teresa. 'It's because we've never seen television before,' she said. 'We don't have it in h—'

'– hour dorms!' Gaby interrupted her quickly.

'Just as well, I should think!' Sister Teresa said.

She did some vigorous knee-bends. 'I'm rounding everyone up for a cross-country run. Collect your shorts and trainers and meet me outside by the school minibus in five minutes. And no excuses, please!'

As she jogged off, Gaby, Angie and Julia made faces and exchanged groans.

'I *hate* running,' said Gaby.

'So do I,' agreed Angie. 'It makes my ringlets all tangled and me all puffed out.'

Julia said, 'But couldn't you . . . you know . . . ?' and she pointed up to the sky.

'Oh, of course!' Gaby said, getting quickly to her feet. 'Come on, you two. See you outside!'

Five minutes later most of Form 1C were standing by the school minibus, dressed in their PE kits and looking less than enthusiastic at the thought of a run.

Gaby examined the minibus with interest. 'It's a pity we're not going – I wouldn't mind a ride in that.'

'Does it fly?' Angie asked Julia.

'Only over bumps in the road,' Julia giggled. 'Don't you have cars? Isn't there any transport at all in heaven?'

Angie shook her head. 'There's no need. Everyone's got wings.'

'Besides, one cloud looks pretty much like the next one,' Gaby said. 'If you go anywhere it's just the same as where you've come from.'

Sister Teresa came up. 'We're being driven five miles to the other side of the park and then we'll run back,' she said. 'If we keep up a good pace all the way home we should make it in one hour.'

The class groaned. Gaby looked at Angie and winked. 'I'm afraid it looks like rain, Sister Teresa.'

Sister Teresa looked up. 'Yes, I believe it does. Oh, what a nuisance,' she said.

Angie sighed. 'Oh, we may not be able to have the lovely run. Oh *dear*.'

'Such a pity,' Gaby said with a long sigh.

'I was so –' Angie began.

Sister Teresa clapped her hands. 'There are plenty of trees where one can shelter – and a little rain never did anyone any harm. If it rains you can run right through it! All aboard the minibus, everyone!'

'Ooh, look, a cat in a tree with a bushy tail,' Angie said as they got out of the minibus.

'That's a squirrel!' Julia said.

'And a huge big black-and-white cat in a field!'

'That's a *cow*!' said Julia, looking round to make sure no one could hear.

'Really? So many different types of cat!' Angie marvelled.

'Ready, everyone?' Sister Teresa called. 'I'll go first and be pathfinder!'

Most of the girls set off, muttering and groaning under their breath.

'Don't get left behind!' Sister Teresa said to Julia, Gaby and Angie, because the three of them were hanging back.

They started – but stopped when they got to the first large bush.

'Sorry about this,' Gaby said to Julia. 'Can you catch the others up?'

'Why?' Julia asked.

'It's like this,' Gaby said, opening her wings and doing a few preliminary flutters in the air. 'Why bother running back when you can fly?'

'I still don't understand how you got back to school so quickly,' Marcy said when they were in the common room that evening. 'I don't remember you passing us.'

'We found a bit of a short cut and got the wind behind us,' Gaby said.

'Our feet hardly touched the ground,' said Angie truthfully.

Sarah came in, looking upset. 'I've just been up to the dorm and my bracelet's gone missing,' she said. 'It's the gold one I had for my birthday.'

Marcy

looked hard at the angels. 'You two were back here ages before anyone else this afternoon!' she said.

'We watched television,' Gaby said.

'And we didn't go up to the dorm at all!' cried Angie.

'That's what *you* say,' said Marcy.

'I *always* tell the truth,' Angie began grandly, 'because I'm –'

Tiblet and Felix the cats, who'd been sitting by Angie's feet, suddenly stood up and arched their backs. Tiblet gave a short yowl.

'I don't think they like Marcy talking to you like that!' Julia said.

Angie looked at Gaby. 'It's the ghost,' she said in an angel-whisper. 'Tiblet's just told me she's coming in!'✻

The Blue Nun wafted through the door, looking very pleased with herself. 'Usually I can only manage to get as far as the main corridor,' she said, 'but I used all my ghostly powers to come and find you.'

✻ Angels can speak and understand animal language.

The cats ran to the far end of the room and crept under a chair, but everyone else carried on chatting, eating or watching TV. The Blue Nun had a few tries at scaring girls, making ghastly faces at Marcy and leaping up and down in front of Sarah, but no one except the angels could see her.

She glided towards the window, looking put out. 'You said you were going to be terrified when you saw me next,' she reminded Angie.

'Sorry,' Angie said in an angel-whisper. 'I forgot.'

'What?' said the ghost.

'She can't hear angel-whispers because she's not an angel,' Gaby said. 'I want to ask her some- thing, though. Let's go out- side.'

They got up and beckoned to the ghost to go out with them.

'I meant to ask you the other night,' Gaby said. 'Have you been taking things from our dorm – chocolates and biscuits and a bracelet?'

The Blue Nun was so incensed that she floated several feet in the air. 'Certainly not!' she said. 'Do you think I'm one of those common ghosts who just move things around? I've never been so insulted in my life!'

8

The Archangel Appeareth

'So, if it isn't the ghost,' Gaby said to Angie, 'then it must be someone else stealing things.'

Angie blinked. 'But who, though? Who would take things from other girls in the dorm?'

'Can't you guess?'

Angie looked thoughtful. 'Now, let me see. In stories on television, it's always the last person you think it's going to be.' She frowned deeply. 'This is just a guess: Mother Superior?'

Gaby rolled her eyes. 'Of course it isn't her! It's probably Marcy.'

'But why would she steal things?'

'To blame it on us and try to get us into trouble, of course. She doesn't like us, does she?'

'No, she doesn't,' Angie said, 'but I don't know why. People are supposed to love angels.' She stood neatly in an angelic attitude, hands clasped and head lowered. *'See an angel, have no fear, Good luck will follow you all year.'*

'But she doesn't *know* she's seen an angel, does she?' Gaby said. 'Mind you, even if she did, I don't think it would make any difference.'

It was lunchtime and Gaby and Angie (having been banned by Miss Bunce from watching TV before afternoon class) were sitting outside on the grass in the sunshine, recovering from that morning's lessons.

Wherever the angels went, animals tended to gather. The cats weren't prowling around right then, so three mice were sitting nearby, nibbling on some cheese Angie had brought out of the dining room. A small flock of sparrows were pecking at the roll Gaby held in her hand, and, because she'd taken off her shoes, a family of spiders had begun to use them for web-spinning exercise.

'So what shall we do about her – about Marcy?' Angie asked.

'Don't know.' Gaby yawned. 'Wait and see what happens, I suppose. No one else in the dorm really thinks it's us who's taking things.'

'*Angels!*' boomed a voice, and Gaby and Angie sat up to attention.

'The Archangel!' Angie squealed, patting her ringlets into place and checking her nails for pearliness.

'But where's the mirror out here?' Gaby wondered aloud.

'Look ye over yonder!'

Turning in the direction of the voice, the angels saw the shimmering figure of the Archangel in a darkened school window. They exchanged horrified looks, then jumped up and ran over to the Archangel, scattering mice, birds and spiders in all directions.

'It seemeth to me that you have been avoiding mirrors,' the Archangel said reproachfully. 'I had to use this outside reflective substance in order to seek you.'

Even Gaby knew better than to tell him lies. 'Well, we have been avoiding you a *bit*,' she said, 'because we've been so busy.'

'It's not that we didn't want to see you,' Angie put in nervously. 'It's just that we had various things going on down here and we were also following three TV series and didn't want to be whisked back to heaven in the middle of them – not that it isn't absolutely wonderful up there,' she finished hastily.

'It is *most* wonderful and glorious,' the Archangel said, a slight note of rebuke in his voice, 'and it is where every virtuous and beauteous angel longs to be.'

Angie coughed. 'Oh, well, we do long to be there, of course . . .'

'. . . but not just at the moment,' Gaby finished. 'Please, Archangel, do let us stay a bit longer.'

'As I have told you before, what you are requesting is against the rules!' the Archangel cried. 'You should be in the celestial kingdom learning to trail clouds of glory – not down here watching some infernal viewing box.'

'We don't just watch a viewing box,' Gaby said, 'we have lessons and learn things.' She nudged Angie to get her to help her out.

'Yes, we learn how to do things like needlework!' Angie said. 'Yesterday it was lazy-daisy stitch. That's useful, isn't it?' she said uncertainly.

'Could we, perhaps,' Gaby wheedled, 'learn to trail clouds of glory down here instead?'

'I've never heard of

such a thing in all my death!' said the Archangel, and then he seemed to relent a little and said more gently, 'You may thinkest heaven rather . . . er . . . slow on Level Six, the level you are on now, but when you learneth more and proceedeth to higher levels it will become much more interesting.'

'But we –' Gaby began – and then there was a sudden fanfare of trumpets from somewhere behind the Archangel. He frowned.

'I cannot stop now. The heavenly host have arrived for harp practice. I'll be back shortly, and meanwhile I'll arrange for a guardian angel to watch over you.'

'What does that mean exactly?' Gaby asked, hoping that they weren't going to have a guardian angel following them about all the time they were on earth.

'It doth not mean she will be on earth with you,' said the Archangel, who had every heavenly art perfected and so knew what the angels were thinking. 'It means someone will be watching over you. If you wanteth anything, then go to a mirror, sing two verses of "Angels from the Realms of Glory" and your guardian angel will appear.'

The Archangel disappeared, looking stern in a radiant and glorious sort of way, and a moment later the school bell rang for afternoon lessons.

The angels, talking glumly about how much longer they could keep the Archangel at bay, went to get their books from their lockers. While they were standing around waiting for Julia, there was a sudden 'Whoo-ooo!' from behind the lockers, and the ghost of the Blue Nun floated into view.

'Oh, not *you* again!' Angie groaned. Julia, who'd just arrived on the scene, blinked and looked hurt.

'I didn't mean *you*,' Angie said hastily.

'It's just the ghost,' Gaby explained.

'Oh, where?!' Julia asked eagerly, but although she strained and squinted and tried terribly hard to see the

ghost, she couldn't see a thing.

'I can materialise in the daytime now!' the ghost said cheerfully. 'It's quite an achievement.'

'Oh, brilliant,' Gaby said.

'You'll be pleased when I tell you what I know!' the ghost said. 'Marcy is in your dormitory at this moment and she's up to something!'

'What's that, then?' Gaby asked.

'What's *what*?' asked Julia, who naturally couldn't hear the ghost. 'Where's the ghost and what are you talking about?'

'Marcy has taken your friend Julia's hairbrush and hidden it under her own mattress,' said the Blue Nun. 'When she lifted the mattress, I saw she had lots of other things hidden under there already.'

'What's she up to then?' Angie asked.

'Can't you guess?' Gaby said to Angie. 'Come on – let's get up there and catch her at it!'

9

The Real Thief

When Gaby and Angie peeped round the door of the dorm, they saw Marcy looking rather pleased with herself, putting school books into her bag. She jumped when she saw the angels.

'What d'you want?' she asked sharply.

'Oh, we just want to check up on something,' Gaby replied.

'Something someone told us about you,' Angie added.

'Well, if it's about me,' Marcy said, 'then it's none of your business.'

'Oh, excuse me, but it *is* our business,' Angie said, 'because you've been stealing things, haven't you? Stealing them and hiding them under your mattress.'

Marcy's jaw dropped in amazement.

'And you've just taken Julia's hairbrush!' Gaby put in.

Marcy, shocked, sank down on to the nearest bed. 'Wha– I don't know what you're talking about,' she blustered.

'I think you do,' Angie said, 'because you've only just taken it.' She crossed the room and heaved up

Marcy's mattress to reveal a box of mint creams, a packet of chocolate biscuits, a gold bracelet and a silver-backed hairbrush. 'There they all are!' she said.

'But how –' Marcy stuttered.

'But how did we find out?' Gaby asked. 'Wouldn't you like to know!'

'Whoo-oouldn't you like to know!' the ghost – who'd followed them upstairs – suddenly shrieked.

Marcy started and shivered. 'Wh . . . what was that?'

Gaby looked at Angie. 'She heard that!'

'Heard what? Did you hear it? What was it?' Marcy asked in confusion, looking all round her.

'Nothing!' Gaby said.

'Just a gho-o-st!' hooted the ghost.

'What was *that*?!' Marcy croaked in fright.

The angels tried not to giggle.

'Why have you been trying to get us into trouble?' Angie asked.

'Because I wanted to,' Marcy said, her eyes darting around the room. 'I think there's something

77

funny about you two. I think –'

She suddenly stopped speaking and went pale. 'Oooh . . . er . . .' she quavered, pointing. 'Wha . . .' But she was so frightened she couldn't get the words out.

'Oh, do stop showing off!' Gaby said to the Blue Nun, who was gliding about the dorm, putting all the things Marcy had stolen back in the lockers where they belonged.

Marcy couldn't see the ghost – she could only see objects floating about all over the room. She jumped up in fright. 'There's something weird going on!' she shouted. 'It's magic! And you're doing it!'

'No, we're not actually,' Angie said mildly.

'All those spooky things happening – you're behind them!'

'No, it's meeeee!'
squealed the ghost,
blowing on the back
of Marcy's neck and
making her jump.

'I'm going downstairs and I'm going to tell everyone about you!' Marcy said, running to the door.

'If you do that,' said Gaby, 'then they'll have to know that it's you who's been stealing their things.'

Marcy stopped in her tracks. 'Well, I'm getting out of here anyway,' she said, and she shot the angels a hateful, fearful look and slammed the door hard behind her. This did not stop the ghost, of course, who stepped neatly through it and followed Marcy down the stairs.

'Now what shall we do?' Angie asked when Marcy's footsteps died away.

'Nothing,' Gaby shrugged. 'We'll just leave everyone to find out that they've got their things back. Marcy won't say anything – she won't dare.'

'And being haunted jolly well serves her right,' Angie said. '*Naughty things you do and say, Come back to you another day*,' she chanted. 'And don't let's have her at our midnight feast next week, either!'

Sister Gertrude, the Maths and Science teacher, was

a very strict, proper nun with deep frown lines on her face and a mouth which looked as if she'd been sucking lemons. The two angels were exactly twenty-seven seconds late for Maths, which made Sister Gertrude very cross. So cross that she decided to give everyone in the class a test.

'I've been working on one of my special little quizzes for some time,' she said slyly. 'It's a nice difficult one with twenty questions to it.'

The class groaned and shuffled their feet.

'Moaning means more homework!' Sister Gertrude snapped, and the class immediately fell silent.

She smiled a sour-lemon smile. 'You will start off with the figure 8765. You will multiply it and divide it and decimalise it and do everything else to it that I specify in the test paper. I want to know the final figure you arrive at – the figure I have written on my pad here. And anyone who gets it wrong will miss TV for the evening and write me an essay entitled: *Why Maths Is My Favourite Lesson*.'

Sister Gertrude passed round the test papers

while the girls exchanged looks of horror. Of everyone in the room, only Felix, sitting on the window sill in the sunshine, appeared perfectly unruffled and content . . .

Which gave Angie an idea. Under her breath she whispered to the cat to come closer, then while everyone was reading through the paper and muttering worriedly, asked Felix very nicely if he'd mind walking along the window sill, looking at Sister Gertrude's pad for the number, then coming back and telling her what it was.

Felix gave a short mew to say yes, he could do that easily. There was nothing to it, he said, it was a piece of mouse.

Sister Gertrude went back to her desk and everyone started scribbling like mad. Felix stretched, yawned and began to tread delicately along the window sill.

'Where's Felix going?' Gaby angel-whispered.

'To get us the answer!' Angie whispered back.

The angels watched as Felix reached the window sill by Sister Gertrude's desk. They saw him arch

his neck delicately in the direction
of the pad – *then* they saw him suddenly leap off the table with a
yowl, his hair standing on
end, and run to hide under a
desk at the back of the class.

A moment later they knew
why: the ghost of the Blue Nun came in – faint
and transparent but smiling and very pleased with
herself.

'Here I am again!' she said, bobbing backwards
and forwards in front of Sister Gertrude's desk.
'Now I can materialise in the daytime I'll be able to
see a lot more of you.'

'Oh, great,' Gaby muttered. 'You do realise that
you've just scared the cat half to death, don't you?'

'Now he won't give us the answer to the test!'
Angie wailed.

'What's that? Who's talking?' Sister Gertrude
snapped. 'You two new girls at the back there –
you can write out your multiplication tables for me
three times!'

'And I'm getting really good at moving things, too!' the Blue Nun said, and she pushed the pile of books that Sister Gertrude was marking and made them fall, one by one, on to the floor.

'What's happening? This class is completely out of order!' Sister Gertrude shouted as the books she was marking began to slide away in all directions and her pens rolled across the floor. 'As well as the essay, everyone can copy their multiplication tables out three times – you two new girls, do yours six times!'

'Thanks a lot!' Gaby said to the ghost.

'You!' Sister Gertrude shrieked at Gaby, 'you do yours *twelve* times for being sarcastic.'

Gaby thought about telling Sister Gertrude that she hadn't been speaking to her, she'd been speaking to the ghost, but in the end she decided not to bother.

That ghost, she decided, was more trouble that it was worth. That ghost, in fact, would have to go . . .

10

Knocking on Heaven's
Door . . .

It was the last lesson of the day and Mother
Superior had just come into the First Years' classroom to take them for singing. She clanged two
cymbals together with such a crash that Gaby and
Angie, sitting at the back and chatting, jumped
with fright.

'Exciting news!' Mother Superior brayed. 'I've
written another verse for the school song!'

Gaby, Angie and the rest of Form 1C did their
best to look excited.

'It's about clapping your troubles right out of the

window! I'm going to write the words on the blackboard, with the chorus, and I want everyone to sing it until they know it through and through.'

She waved her tambourine towards Angie. 'I've been taking music lessons!' she said, jigging around as if she had itching powder in her habit. 'I can sing much better now.'

'Well, you certainly couldn't sing any worse,' Angie said kindly.

The class looked at Mother Superior anxiously but she just chortled. She began to write the school song on the blackboard.

Julia watched and as soon as the chorus with its *Banish every thought of hell* came up, she turned and whispered to Gaby. 'I really don't think I can keep sneezing for the rest of the lesson,' she said, 'so I'm going to pretend to faint. You and Angie can carry me out.' And with that she sighed loudly and collapsed in a heap on to her desk.

Angie looked at her in surprise. 'Has she had angel dust?' she asked Gaby.

''Course not,' Gaby said. 'She just wants to get out.' She raised her hand. 'Please, Mother Superior, Julia's fainted. May Angie and I take her out for some fresh air?'

Once outside the classroom, the three girls made their way along the corridors and up the stairs to their dorm.

'I wanted to get out early anyway,' Julia said, bouncing down on her bed, 'because we need to plan the midnight feast. Has anyone got an alarm clock?'

'We won't need a clock,' Angie said. 'I'll get Tiblet to wake us up. The cats are always awake at night – Felix told me they usually have a midnight feast themselves.'

Gaby nodded. 'They have theirs in the kitchen dustbins, though.'

'Yuk,' Julia said. 'Don't ask them to bring any food with them, will you?'

Angie opened her locker and a brown paper bag bobbed towards her. 'We've made some more angel cakes,' she said. The bag started drifting away and she made a grab for it. 'Sister Bridget told us she'd never seen cakes as light as ours.'

'And she said we could make them whenever we liked,' Gaby went on, 'just as long as we let her have half.'

'I've got a tin of biscuits,' Julia said, 'and I know Susie's got some brandy snaps and Sarah's got a box of candied fruit.' She hesitated. 'The thing is — what are we going to do about Marcy?'

Both angels pulled faces.

'Does she *have* to come?' Angie asked.

'No one wants her, but she's bound to wake up,' Julia said.

'She's still being nasty,' Angie complained. 'She called us the spook sisters this morning.'

'So what can we do about her?' Julia asked.

'How about,' Gaby said, 'a little light sprinkling of angel dust on her pillow . . . ?'

It was midnight. Marcy was snoring gently and Felix and Tiblet (smelling only slightly of dustbin) had arrived in the dorm to wake the girls.

The others didn't know that Marcy had angel dust sprinkled on her pillow and were worried she'd wake up, so Susie suggested they went to the common room downstairs. Julia nodded. 'Good idea. We'll be miles away from Miss Bunce down there.'

'*And* we can watch the late-night film!' Angie added gleefully.

Accompanied by the cats, they tiptoed out of the dorm and went downstairs with their bags of goodies.

'Shall we let the cakes float down on their own?' Angie angel-whispered.

'Silly,' Gaby said. 'They'd get lost on the way.'

Sarah said they shouldn't put the light on in the common room in case Miss Bunce or one of the nuns saw it, so instead they opened the curtains to let in the moonlight and Susie stood her torch on the table. They spread the food on the floor and Angie turned on the television, very low.

Sarah poured everyone a paper cup of lemonade.

'Happy midnight feast, everyone!' she said, and they were all drinking to that when the cats suddenly leapt for cover, sending the lemonade flying and knocking a brandy snap out of Angie's hand. With a yowl of terror they hurled themselves under the settee.

'What's wrong with *them*?' Sarah asked.

Gaby and Angie exchanged glances.

'Oh, not *again*,' Gaby angel-whispered. 'I'm getting fed up with her.'

'Hasn't she got anything better to do with herself?'

The ghost of the Blue Nun floated through the door. 'This looks fun,' she said. 'Mind if I join you?'

'Yes, we do, actually,' Gaby angel-whispered. 'You're really beginning to be a bit of pain with your sudden appearances.'

'We might just as well have a guardian angel following us about,' muttered Angie.

'That gives me an idea,' Gaby angel-whispered to Angie. 'Let's go back to the dorm . . .'

Pretending to the others that they'd left some food behind (and giving Julia the bag of angel cakes to hold down), the angels went outside, followed closely by the Blue Nun.

'What's happening? Where are we going now?' she asked. 'Can I come?'

'Of course,' Gaby said. 'In fact, we've got a special surprise for you.'

'Beat you up to the dorm!' Angie said, and the two angels slipped their wings out and flew up the stairs with the ghost, round and round to the top of the tower.

'All these new things I can do!' boasted the ghost. 'I can float all over the show, I can come out in daytime, I can move things – and if I try really hard I can make someone hear me!' She smiled smugly. 'I've been learning all sorts of new ghostly skills: anything an angel can do, I can do just as well.'

'Hmm,' Gaby said, 'we'll see about that.'

'Why have you come back up to your dormitory?' the ghost asked. 'Is there someone here I can scare?'

They floated across to the sleeping form of Marcy. 'You can scare her as much as you like,' Gaby said, 'but I don't think she'll notice. No, come and see our bathroom . . .'

'Oh!' Angie winked at Gaby. 'I get it.'

The Blue Nun, Gaby and Angie went into the bathroom and stood in a line in front of the mirror.

'Now, how would you like to see a guardian angel?' Gaby asked the ghost.

'Mmm,' said the Blue Nun, considering. 'I wouldn't mind. Would I be able to scare it at all?'

The angels didn't reply, they just began singing 'Angels from the Realms of Glory' most beautifully.

As the second verse died away, a guardian angel appeared, bright as a star in the mirror before them. They all stepped back a pace. The guardian angel was not as magnificent a spectacle as the Archangel, being not quite so splendidly winged, but she was quite magnificent enough to stun the Blue Nun and our two angels into awed silence.

'Three celestial beings!' cried the guardian angel.

'I've only been watching over two.'

The angels bowed their heads. 'We found an extra one,' Angie murmured humbly.

'And she wants to come back to heaven!' Gaby cried.

Eager at the thought of getting rid of the Blue Nun, they gave her a gentle push towards the mirror. They stepped back to enjoy watching her disappear . . . but just at that moment old Sister Bertha pushed open the bathroom door.

Her habit was ruffled, as if she'd put it on in a hurry. She blinked like an owl as she looked around her. 'I heard heavenly voices singing and saw a bright light,' she said wonderingly. 'What's happening in here?'

Her gaze locked on to the glorious figure of the guardian angel in the mirror and her jaw dropped. As if in a trance, she moved towards it. All at once, a strange misty glow swirled out of the mirror. It surrounded the Blue Nun and Sister Bertha, swished around them and seemed to gather them up in the mirror. As the angels watched, dumb-

struck, the guardian angel, the Blue Nun and Sister
Bertha all disappeared.

Gaby and Angie gave little screams.

'Sister Bertha, come back!' Gaby called in a
panic.

'Oh, no!' Angie gasped. 'She's gone up with the
ghost!'

'Gone to heaven!' squealed Gaby. 'And she's not even dead!'

The angels looked at each other in fright.

'We're going to get into the most terrible trouble,' said Gaby.

'The Archangel will never forgive us.'

'You're right,' Gaby sighed. 'He'll go all out to get us back now.'

'What shall we do?'

'Well,' Gaby said after a moment's thought, 'I suggest we go back to the midnight feast and eat as much as we can. After all, it might be the last meal we have on earth . . .'

Is there An Angel in Your School?

Here's a quick 'Angel spotter' guide. If you can answer *yes* to any of the questions, you score 2 points.

1. Has anyone ever come to school wearing a nightie?
2. Does anybody *regularly* talk to animals?
3. Are there people who say 'just flying off to see . . .'
4. Smell or what? Is there anyone who *never* washes behind their ears or . . . backs?

5. Have you ever seen anyone who can jump suspiciously high *and* stay up?

If your total score is between 6–10:

No way! You may well have a real-life angel at school! Invite them home to tea – now! (Don't forget to serve angel cake.)

If your total score is between 2–6:

Well, it's possible, or you may just have flighty (or smelly) friends. Try saying 'halo halo' to them (instead of 'hallo hallo') and see if they look shifty.

If your total score is between 0–2:

Sad to say, it looks pretty unlikely you've got angels at your school. Still, you could always pretend and look out for Mary Hooper's next TWO NAUGHTY ANGELS adventure, ROUND THE RAINBOW!

Don't miss the next
Two Naughty Angels
adventure:

Round the Rainbow

Available now!

Turn the page for a taster of what's to come in
an excerpt from the opening chapter . . .

A Flying Start

Gaby wriggled her wings, opened them out fully and rose a few feet into the air.

'Oh, that's better! It's so nice to stretch your wings,' she said.

Angie fluttered hers and joined Gaby halfway up a tree. 'It is, isn't it?' she said. 'It does them no good at all to be squashed under a vest all day.'

Gaby and Angie had come out to the school field to have a bit of a fly around – and also to decide what to do about Sister Bertha, a teacher at their school who'd gone to heaven before her time.

'Well, it wasn't *our* fault,' Angie said. 'We didn't know Sister Bertha would come into our dorm just when the guardian angel appeared, did we?'

'It doesn't matter whose fault it was,' Gaby said gloomily, 'Sister Bertha is where she shouldn't be and we're going to get into awful trouble' – she pointed upwards – '*you know where.*'

'Upstairs in the dorms?' Angie asked.

'Upstairs in heaven, silly!' Gaby said. 'What do you think the Archangel is going to say about someone arriving from earth who isn't dead? It's strictly against the rules.'

'Well,' Angie said earnestly, 'can't we just explain to him that we sent the school ghost back to heaven where she belonged . . .'

'Back to a lower level than *ours*, of course!' put in Gaby, who was a bit snobbish about ghosts.

'And then just explain to him that Sister Bertha

accidentally went too,' Angie continued.

'That's as may be,' Gaby said, as she reached up to take an apple from the branch, 'but the fact is we've messed up the right order of things and he's going to be *very cross*.'

Angie nodded thoughtfully. 'I suppose if it hadn't been for our heavenly singing, Sister Bertha wouldn't have come up in the middle of the night and found us.' She sighed. 'We're *never* going to get our haloes back now!'✻

'I never had one in the first place,' said Gaby – who was rather naughtier than Angie.

Angie gave a smug smile. 'Well, you never went to Halo Awareness Classes, did you?'

✻ Angels have to earn their haloes – the better they are, the brighter the haloes.

'The other thing,' Gaby went on, taking no notice of the dig, 'is that now the Archangel will be even more determined to get us back to heaven.'

'Oh *no*!' Angie sighed again. 'Just think what it should be like if we had to go back: no more television . . .'

'No more animals . . .'

'No more proper food . . .'

'No more midnight feasts . . .'

'No more fun!'

'And what would we get instead?' Gaby groaned. 'Just a whole lot of clouds!' She gave a vast sigh and a few drops of rain fell.

Both angels looked up to the sky. 'Oops,' Angie said. 'We've both been sighing.'✲

'We'd better go in,' Gaby said. 'I hate getting my wings wet.'

'And my ringlets go all frizzy! But what shall we do about Sister Bertha?'

'I think we'll just sit tight and see,' Gaby said.

✲ When angels sigh, storm clouds gather and rain falls.

'Maybe no one will realise she isn't here. Maybe they'll just think she's gone on holiday.'

The angels landed gently on the grass, tucked in their wings and began to walk back to school.

'I don't want to go back to heaven,' Gaby said. 'I'm not ready.'

Angie thought for a moment. 'Nor am I,' she said. 'I wasn't sure at first about coming down here, but now I really like it.'

'I might be ready to go back in a hundred and fifty years or so,' Gaby said, 'but right now I'm enjoying myself too much.'

They went into school – and bumped straight into their form teacher, Miss Bunce.

Miss Bunce was an old dear who'd been at St Winifred's for years and years. She was one of the few teachers who wasn't a nun. Instead of wearing black, she wore a strange assortment of floaty dresses, wispy scarves and brightly coloured shawls. The whole effect was that of a small walking tent.

'Dears!' she said to Gaby and Angie. 'Mother

Superior has called a special meeting in the school hall, and every girl and every teacher has to attend. Run along and tell the other First Years, will you?'

Gaby and Angie nodded politely, but Gaby angel-whispered to Angie, 'What if the meeting's about Sister Bertha?!'※

Angie gave a small shriek of alarm.

'Er . . . what's the meeting about?' Gaby asked Miss Bunce.

'We'll find that out in good time,' Miss Bunce said gently. 'Now, off you go, because Mother Superior wants us there immediately. I'm going up to Sister Bertha's study to tell her about it. Come to think of it, I haven't seen Sister Bertha for

---

※ Angels can speak to each other so softly no one else can hear.

a day or so,' she murmured as she wandered off.

Gaby and Angie looked at each other.

'Oh *no*!' Gaby said. 'She's going to find out that Sister Bertha's disappeared.'

'So what shall we do now?'

Gaby thought for a moment. 'Come on!' she said, tugging Angie. 'We're going to have to get a bit wet – but it's all in a good cause.'

'Where are we going?'

'Sister Bertha's room!'

Once outside, the angels flapped their wings and in a few seconds had flown up to Sister Bertha's third-floor study. The window, luckily, was open, and they slipped inside.

'Now what?' Angie said. 'Miss Bunce will be here in a minute.'

'We're going to play Sister Bertha!' Gaby said . . .